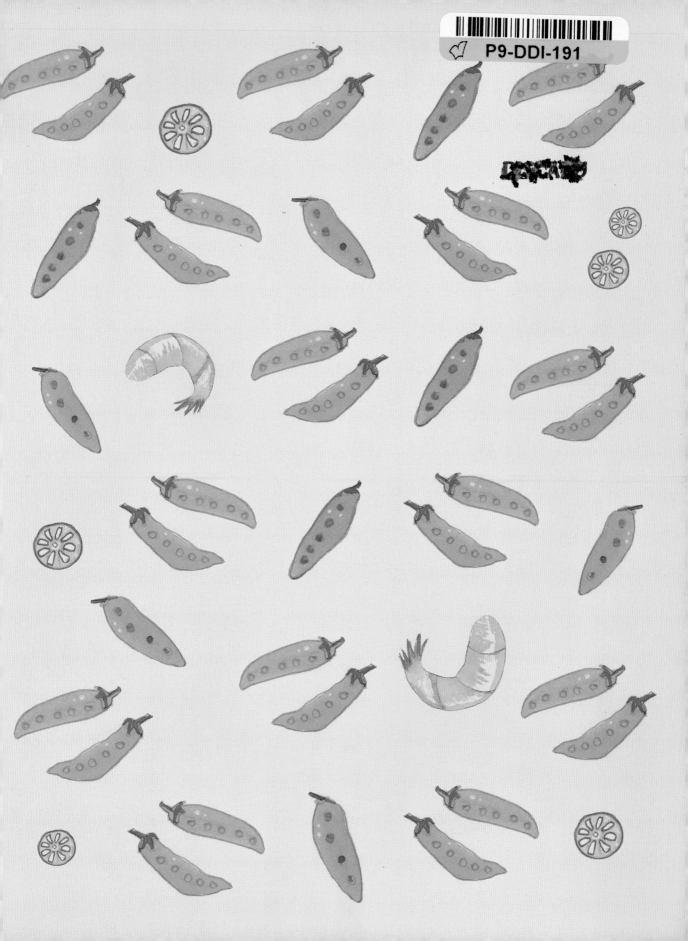

First edition 2019

Library of Congress Catalog Card Number pending
ISBN 978-0-7636-9548-4

19 20 21 22 23 24 CCP 10 9 8 7 6 5 4 3 2 1

Printed in Shenzhen, Guangdong, China

This book was typeset in Maiandra.
The illustrations were done in watercolor and aquarelle pencil.

Candlewick Press
99 Dover Street
Somerville, Massachusetts 02144

visit us at www.candlewick.com

FELIX EATS UP

ROSEMARY WELLS

CANDLEWICK PRESS

Felix brought the same sandwich to school every day.

He had no need to try anything new.

He was happy with just his sprouts on buttered oat bread.

Felix's best friend, Fiona, chowed down on
an enchilada with hot sauce.

"Maybe it's time to widen your food horizons, Felix!"
she said. But Felix did not want to.

During After-Lunch Recycle Moment, Fiona
reminded Felix, "Tonight's the night you sleep over!"

"Oh, yes!" said Felix. "Your mama will make my favorite
macaroni and cheese for me as she always does!"

After lunch, it was time for Miss B's students
to create their leaf collections.

"Today is my half birthday, and we are going
to a restaurant," whispered Fiona.

Miss B gave Felix a gold star for his Red Maple Medley, but Felix was worrying about eating out.

He hoped they would go to Gino's. Gino's served pasta with butter. Pasta with butter was no problem.

Everyone put on their bird hats and picked up their whistles for birdcall time.

But through the chirping and whistling, Felix worried.

"Do you think we'll go to Gino's?" Felix asked Fiona.

"Nope!" said Fiona. "We're tired of pasta! Maybe the Sausage and Mashed Shack instead."

Felix did not eat sausage or mashed. Mashed what?

And the sausages might have liver in them.

On the way home, Fiona said, "On the other hand, maybe we'll go to the Fish and Chips House!"

Felix had never tried fish or chips. He didn't like the sound of it.

"You look worried, Felix!"

"I'm not worried a bit," said Felix.

"Did you bring your sleeping bear and your Softie the Snowman pajamas?" asked Fiona.

"All packed," said Felix.

"Then there's nothing to worry about," said Fiona.

At the front door, Fiona's mama was
waiting with buttered carrot muffins.

"These muffins have spots," whispered Felix.

Fiona took the pistachios and raisins out of Felix's muffin for him.

All of a sudden, Fiona's mama called the Dragon's Belly. She made a reservation for four.

Felix froze. The Dragon's Belly was sure to serve peppers so hot your teeth could catch fire!

"Yay!" said Fiona.

To Felix, Fiona said, "You can have egg drop soup. Egg drop soup has no taste, no peppers, and no bits in it."

Still, Felix knew he wouldn't like it.

At the Dragon's Belly, the waiter took their orders.

"The Crab Dreamboat, please," said Fiona's daddy.

"Buddha's Delight, please," said Fiona's mama.

"I'd like moo shu pancakes, please," said Fiona.
"They're my favorite!"

"Mac and cheese, please," Felix said softly.

"I beg your pardon?" said the waiter.

"He said snow peas, please," said Fiona.

Felix knew the snow peas would be served
in a mound of ice.

But the waiter brought warm
pearly-green snow peas.

"Open wide, Felix!" Fiona said.

Felix closed his eyes. Fiona dropped
a snow pea into his mouth.

There was no getting around it: the snow pea was delicious.

It tasted like a kiss of summertime sun.

Felix ate them all. When he finished eating, he wanted more.

"Now try this," said Fiona. "It's a mushroom."

"I don't like mushrooms," said Felix.

"Have you ever tasted one?"

Felix took a deep breath. The mushroom tasted wonderful.

Then Felix tried eggplant, lotus root, red melon, and bok choy. He gobbled down taro root, Chinese cabbage, bean cake, water chestnuts, and shrimp egg roll. Then he made short work of a claw from the Crab Dreamboat!

"Felix!" said Fiona. "You've just eaten twelve new things!"

The waiter brought birthday-candle
fortune cookies to the table.

Everyone sang the half-birthday song
to Fiona.

They sang it all the way home in the car, and
all the way to bedtime.

"Tomorrow," said Felix, "I'm going to take
leftover moo shu pancakes to school for lunch."

"Felix," asked Fiona, "what was in
your fortune cookie?"

But Felix was already fast asleep.

Your horizons go all the way to China

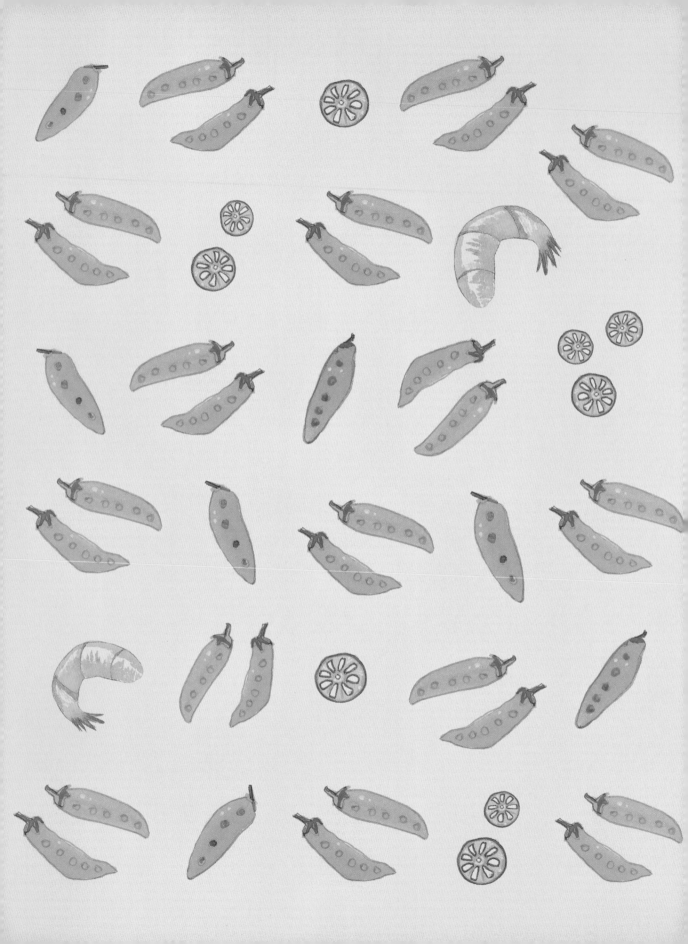